Cougar
Frenzy

Cougar Frenzy

Pamela McDowell

illustrated by
Kasia Charko

orca Echoes

ORCA BOOK PUBLISHERS

Library and Archives Canada Cataloguing in Publication

Title: Cougar frenzy / Pamela McDowell; illustrated by Kasia Charko.
Names: McDowell, Pamela, author. | Charko, Kasia, illustrator.
Series: Orca echoes.

Description: Series statement: Orca echoes

Identifiers: Canadiana (print) 201900658oX | Canadiana (ebook) 20190065834 |
ISBN 9781459820647 (softcover) | ISBN 9781459820654 (PDF) |
ISBN 9781459820661 (EPUB)

Classification: LCC PS8625.D785 C68 2019 | DDC jC813/.6—dc23

Library of Congress Control Number: 2019934029
Simultaneously published in Canada and the United States in 2019

*Orca Book Publishers is committed to reducing the consumption of
nonrenewable resources in the making of our books. We make every
effort to use materials that support a sustainable future.*

Summary: In this illustrated early chapter book, Cricket has to convince the
townspeople of Waterton, located in the heart of Waterton Lakes National Park, not
to capture and relocate a cougar that they believe is being a nuisance.

Orca Book Publishers gratefully acknowledges the support for its publishing
programs provided by the following agencies: the Government of Canada,
the Canada Council for the Arts and the Province of British Columbia through
the BC Arts Council and the Book Publishing Tax Credit.

Edited by Liz Kemp
Cover artwork and interior illustrations by Kasia Charko
Author photo by Mirror Image Photography

ORCA BOOK PUBLISHERS
orcabook.com

Printed and bound in Canada.

22 21 20 19 • 4 3 2 1

For Lori, whose story of a cougar on Crandell Lake Trail sparked my imagination.

Chapter One

"Look out below!"

Cricket jumped back into the house as a giant slab of snow slid off the roof. *Wump!* It landed in a heap, blocking the sidewalk.

She poked her head out the front door. "Good one, Tyler!" she yelled. "Now how am I supposed to get to school?"

Tyler laughed, and she slammed the door, sending another hunk of snow crashing to the ground. Cricket's older brother was twelve, and it was his job to climb up on the roof to shovel off the heavy snow.

She opened the back door quietly, then dashed down the steps into the yard. Nearly three feet of snow had fallen in the past week, and the little village of Waterton was hiding under a heavy white blanket. Everything was soft and round and quiet. She followed the path her dad had made with the plow on the front of his truck. Warden McKay was a park warden in Waterton Lakes National Park, and part of his job was making sure the roads were safe in the winter.

"Hey, Cricket! C'mon!" Cricket's best friend, Shilo, was waiting on the corner. "If we're late, Mr. Tanaka will make us sort the recycling again."

Cricket wrinkled her nose. "Ew!"

"I know," Shilo said. "That's almost worse than scraping the bat poop out of our shed."

"No, not that." Cricket covered her nose with her mitten as they walked. "Don't you smell something? It's getting stronger."

Shilo sniffed the air. "Must be a skunk. C'mon, let's go."

"Wait, Shilo. Look!" Cricket pointed to a bush in the corner of the school field. "Somebody piled a bunch of snow under that bush."

"Some kids probably made a fort."

"I don't think so. See all the scratch marks in the snow? And the branches and dead leaves? Somebody tried to hide something under there—something smelly."

Shilo frowned and pulled her scarf up over her nose.

"I think somebody hid their dinner under that bush." Cricket looked up at the ravens in the trees above them. "We shouldn't be this close."

"Do you think it was a bear? Or a wolf?" Shilo looked around nervously.

Cricket shook her head. "We better get to school and call my dad." She grabbed Shilo's arm to stop her from running.

"You have to walk."

"What—? What do you think it was?"

"A cougar," Cricket said, looking over her shoulder. "I think it was a cougar."

* * *

Mr. Tanaka led the fourth-grade students into the school gym. The entire school population was seated on the floor, buzzing with curiosity. What was going on? Were they having a special presentation? Cricket and Shilo followed Mr. Tanaka and sat with their classmates.

"Hey, Cricket, there's your dad. He got here quick," Shilo said.

Principal Singh stepped to the front of the gym. She waited for the students to stop talking, then introduced Warden McKay.

"Good morning, students," he began.

The first-grade kids at the front answered him. "Good morning, Warden McKay."

He smiled, then became very serious. "You all know that we live in a national park. You know that there is wildlife all around us."

Many of the students nodded.

"We have had an unusual visitor. A cougar has been seen in the village." Warden McKay paused as the students began to chatter. Principal Singh held up her hand for quiet.

"In the winter, when the bears are asleep, we sometimes forget that other

dangerous animals live here too. Does anyone know what to do to protect yourself from a cougar?"

Hands shot into the air.

"Never walk alone."

"Never run if you see a cougar."

"Make yourself look bigger," said a fifth-grade student.

Warden McKay nodded. "How would you do that? How would you make yourself look bigger to a cougar?"

The student stood up. "You could open your coat like this," he said, unzipping his sweatshirt and spreading it wide open.

"That's a great example," Warden McKay said. "Are there any other suggestions?"

"I have one," a student called from the back of the gym.

Cricket rolled her eyes. Of course Tyler would have something to say.

"Dusk and dawn mean dinner," Tyler said.

"What does he mean by that?" Shilo whispered.

Cricket made a face.

Warden McKay nodded. "That's right, Tyler. Cougars hunt at dusk and at dawn, so those are the most dangerous times for you to be out. We should also keep pets indoors and make sure garages and shed doors are closed."

A first-grade student in the front row put up her hand. "Did you see the cougar, Warden McKay?"

He shook his head. "No, Maddy. Cougars are very shy and don't usually like to be around people. I didn't see this cougar, but there is evidence that he has been here, and he may come back."

"You were right," Shilo whispered.

Cricket nodded.

"So for the next couple of days, it is important that you stay safe. Principal Singh has canceled school for the rest of the week, until we know there is no danger."

The students cheered in surprise. Principal Singh never canceled school— not even for a snow day. A cougar was a really big deal.

Chapter Two

After lunch the girls walked down to the gas station for ice cream. Mrs. McKay insisted that Tyler walk with them, though Cricket secretly thought he would attract more cougars than he scared away. The bell above the gas-station door jangled as Cricket opened it.

"Hi, kids." Pat Watson was a tall man with a booming voice. He had owned the only gas station in Waterton for twenty-two years. In the summer he rented bicycles, mopeds and fishing rods to tourists. For the rest of the year townsfolk stopped at the gas station to chat and maybe pick up a new shovel or puzzle or ice-fishing line.

Today the wrangler from the stables was at the counter, buying a bag of beef jerky and chatting with Pat.

"Hi, Mr. Watson. Hi, Mr. Garrin," Cricket said. She and Shilo moved to the

ice-cream cooler. Tyler stopped to check out the model-airplane kits on the top shelf, behind the camp stoves.

Mr. Garrin continued their conversation as Pat handed him his change. "I'm not really surprised," he said. "There was a cougar that caused some trouble around town in the seventies."

The bell jangled, and everyone looked toward the door. A young man entered the garage, nodded to Pat and continued to the back of the store. He was dressed like most hikers and skiers who visited Waterton, with insulated pants and a warm coat, wearing a red, blue and white Montreal Canadiens knit hat on his head.

"There have been some signs around the corrals," Mr. Garrin said. "Something's been stirring up the horses at night, spooking 'em."

Cricket nudged Shilo with her elbow. She watched the young man, who was frowning as he carried a bottle of kerosene to the counter.

"If you don't mind my asking," he said, "did you see what spooked the horses?"

Mr. Garrin shook his head. "Nah. It was too sneaky. It was brown though. Or maybe black. Too small for a bear."

"Did you find any tracks?"

"Nope. The horses stirred up the snow. It had to be a cougar. What else could it be?"

Pat held out a receipt for the kerosene. "It's got to be a cougar, right, Jeremy?"

The young man shrugged slowly and said goodbye. He put the receipt in his pocket and headed out the door.

Jeremy! He was the university researcher studying Waterton's cougars! Cricket's dad had mentioned the project the previous month and had seemed impressed with the equipment the team was using. Cricket jabbed Shilo with her elbow again.

"Ouch! Stop doing that!"

"Come on!"

Pushing Shilo ahead of her, Cricket dragged Tyler out of the store with them.

"Mr. Bowman, wait!" Cricket called. "Do you really think it could be a cougar?"

The man turned and raised his eyebrows.

"We found some evidence this morning," she said, gesturing to Shilo.

He smiled. "Call me Jeremy. You're Warden McKay's daughter, aren't you? You found the dead deer cached in the schoolyard?"

Cricket nodded and introduced herself and Shilo and Tyler. "I've lived here all my life, and I've never seen a cougar," she said.

"Cougars are pretty shy, but they are out there. I'll have to check the signals of all the collared cats and see where they are."

"You put collars on the cougars?" Shilo's voice squeaked. "Isn't that dangerous?"

Jeremy smiled again. "It could be dangerous, but I have lots of help. The collars have radio transmitters that help me keep track of each cougar. I'm researching how far cougars travel in their range." He looked down the street. "I'm heading back to my cabin now. Are you three walking my way?"

Before Shilo could protest that they hadn't bought their ice cream, Cricket nodded and fell into step beside Jeremy. This was their chance to learn more about the cougar!

Chapter Three

"If cougars are so secretive, how do you find one to put a collar on it?" Shilo asked as they walked through the village.

"The best time is right after a snowfall. I go out in the truck with a local guide and some dogs, looking for tracks. When I'm sure they are cougar tracks, we let the dogs off leash, and they follow the scent."

Cricket and Shilo both stared at him, their eyes wide.

"Don't worry, the dogs never catch the cougar. A cougar's like any other cat—he'll climb a tree to get out of reach of trouble. But the dogs will keep him in the tree until we catch up."

"I bet that takes a while," Tyler said.

Jeremy nodded. "That's probably the hardest part of the job, hiking through miles of deep snow. Snowshoes help a bit."

"Doesn't the cougar get mad hanging in the tree with the dogs barking at it?" Cricket asked.

"Yeah, there's a lot of hissing and spitting. But I tranquilize the cougar with a dart gun, and that calms it down."

"Doesn't it fall out of the tree?"

"That's the tricky part. Once the cat quiets down, I have to climb the tree and loop a rope around one of its legs before it falls completely asleep and lets go of the branch."

"I get it," Tyler said. "You can hook the other end of the rope over a branch to let the cougar down gently."

"That's the goal." Jeremy stopped. "Would you like to see my research station? It's in the old Miller cabin on the corner."

Cricket turned to Tyler.

"We better phone Mom," he said. "She'll have a fit if she can't find us."

* * *

Jeremy's cabin was filled with computers and GPS equipment. On one table there were devices that looked like game controllers with long antennas poking out like whiskers. Another table was covered with maps. Some of the maps showed elevation and land features like rivers. Other maps showed roads and property lines.

"Is this a radio collar?" Cricket pointed to a ring of metal the size of a dinner plate and about four inches wide. It was padded on the inside.

"That's right," Jeremy said. He picked up the collar with both hands and opened it. "It's pretty simple to use. You just snap it on like this." He turned to Tyler and put the collar around his neck. "Then you turn the transmitter on with this switch. The GPS unit uses satellites to record the location of the cougar, using latitude and longitude. That data is sent to my computer."

Tyler grimaced. "It's kind of heavy."

"That's the battery. The collar is lightweight by itself."

"Do the collars ever stop working?" Cricket asked. "Do the batteries ever run out?"

"If the battery runs out, the collar opens up and falls off." Jeremy undid the collar and removed it from Tyler's neck.

"So if the cougar at the stables was wearing a collar, you would have that data?"

Jeremy nodded. "That's right. Let's have a look," he said, sitting down in front of a computer.

Cricket looked at the table beside her. A white plaster disc the size of a pie was sitting on the table. She picked it up and turned it over.

Shilo peeked over her shoulder. "Cool! Is that a cougar print?"

Jeremy turned in his chair. "Yup. I made that impression last fall."

Cricket placed her hand over the paw print. She stretched her pinky to reach the far toe.

"Notice anything missing from that print?" Jeremy asked.

Cricket studied the print. There were four toes and the middle heel pad. What was missing?

Tyler stepped over to have a look. "There are no claw marks," he said.

"Right. A cougar keeps its claws retracted unless it's running." Jeremy turned back to his computer. "Hmm, it looks like Elvis was in town."

"Who?"

"Elvis?"

Jeremy looked up and grinned. "There's an old cougar I named Elvis. It looks like he passed through town last night."

"Was he at the school?" Cricket asked.

The kids peered over Jeremy's shoulder at the computer screen.

"That looks like a dot-to-dot puzzle," Shilo said.

Jeremy smiled. "I guess it does. This is the data the GPS collar sends me. Each dot is a 'ping,' and it tells me where the cougar was at that exact moment. Right now the pings are set for every half hour," he explained. "The battery turns on the GPS, connects with the satellites and sends the data to me."

"There are a lot of dots in one spot," Cricket said.

Jeremy enlarged the map. "It looks like he was in the schoolyard for a couple of hours last night."

"What about earlier?" Shilo asked. "Mr. Garrin said he thought the cougar was hanging around the horses. Was it Elvis?"

"I don't think so. He came up from Montana and traveled around Bertha Peak before he came into town." Jeremy traced the bright-green line on the map with his finger. "It doesn't look like he went anywhere near the stables."

"What's the yellow line?" Tyler asked.

"That's Madonna. She's west of Cameron Lake. It would take her a couple of days to get here, and it would be unusual for her to travel this far out of her normal range."

"There's *another* cougar?"

"Yup. Here, have a look." Jeremy closed the satellite map and opened a black-and-white photo on the screen. It showed an adult cougar on a snowy trail in the bush. Its eyes glowed brightly.

"Hey, that's a night-vision picture!" Tyler said. "How did you get that?"

"I set up a motion-activated night-vision camera at Cameron Lake. Cool, eh? And look here." Jeremy pointed to a spot behind the cougar.

Cricket leaned forward to get a better look. "There's another cougar there!"

"Two!" Shilo said. "Are they kittens?"

Jeremy nodded. "That's Hanna and Taylor, Madonna's cubs from last summer. They're getting pretty big now."

The kids grinned. "Wow! Do you have any pictures of Elvis?"

"No. I guess I should move one of my cameras."

"You could put it at the school," Shilo suggested. "Then we can see him when he comes back for the dinner he left in the schoolyard."

Chapter Four

The next morning the phone rang while Cricket was getting dressed. The phone rang two minutes later as she headed down the stairs. It rang again as she spread peanut butter on her toast. She looked up as Warden McKay came into the kitchen with his coffee cup.

"What's happening, Dad?"

He blew out a sigh and shook his head. "The town is caught in a phantom frenzy," he said. "People are seeing this phantom cougar everywhere."

Cricket's heart jumped. "Really?"

"No, not unless he can be three places at one time or all the cougars in the park decided to come to town on the same day. Mrs. Steeves saw something brown on her back deck, someone else reported it in a tree on Waterton Avenue, and Mr. Tanaka heard growling coming from the bushes in his yard."

Cricket turned to look out the kitchen window. Mr. Tanaka lived next door, which meant the cougar might have been right under her bedroom window!

The phone rang again.

"Yes?" Warden McKay frowned. "Didn't they see the signs before they headed out on the trail?"

Cricket stopped eating and watched her dad carefully. When he hung up the phone, he turned to Cricket.

"What happened, Dad?"

"A couple of snowshoers stopped at the station to report cougar tracks on the trail to Bertha Lake. Somehow they didn't see the bright-orange signs closing the trail."

"Are they okay?"

Warden McKay nodded as he transferred his coffee into a travel mug. "They turned back to get a camera from their car and saw paw prints beside their tracks."

Cricket's eyes grew wide. "Was the cougar following them?"

"Maybe, though it's possible it wasn't even a cougar at all." He snapped the lid on his cup. "I'm going to check it out now. Do you want to come for the drive?"

"You bet!" Cricket popped the last crust of toast into her mouth and jumped up to get her coat.

* * *

After he parked the truck, Warden McKay unlocked his rifle from the gun rack above the back seat. Cricket's heart thumped as she watched him check to see that it was loaded. She couldn't remember the last time she had seen him get the gun out.

"Don't worry, Cricket. I don't expect to need this, but it's best to be prepared," he said. Cricket noticed that he didn't strap the rifle to his back—he carried it in his hand instead. Her senses were on high alert, listening for the rustle of branches and watching for any sign of movement around them. Not far up the Bertha Lake Trail, Warden McKay knelt to study tracks that came out of the bush and continued along the trail.

"Do you know how to identify a cougar track?" he asked.

Cricket thought of the plaster model on Jeremy's desk. "It probably won't have claw marks," she said.

Her dad nodded. "That's right. A cougar keeps its claws retracted, but a canine doesn't."

"You mean a canine like a wolf or a dog?"

"Right. And a cougar's toes are shaped a little differently, more like a teardrop." His finger traced a line through the print. "You can draw an X

between the outer toes and the pad of a canine print, but not this one."

Cricket bent down to study the track more closely. "So it really was a cougar following them?"

"It sure looks like it." Warden McKay stood up and brushed the snow from his knee. "I'll need to file a report on this one."

On the way home they drove past the schoolyard.

"Do you think the cougar has been back?" Cricket asked. She described Jeremy's plan to set up a night-vision camera to get a picture of the cougar. Warden McKay stopped the truck, and Cricket studied the bush where she had seen the pile of snow the day before.

"It looks different," she said. "Yesterday everything was hidden under the bush. I knew something was there because I *smelled* it. It wasn't a big mess like this." The deer was no longer buried, and branches and dead leaves had been tossed out onto the snow all around the bush.

"Stay here, Cricket. Don't get out of the truck."

Again her dad unlocked his rifle and carried it with him. She watched as he walked in a wide circle around the bush. He knelt down to study something in the snow and shook his head.

When he climbed back into the truck, he looked bewildered.

"What's the matter, Dad? Was it the cougar? Did you find cougar tracks?"

"No," he said, frowning. "Not cougar tracks—dog tracks. The biggest dog tracks I've ever seen. Even bigger than a wolf."

Cricket sat back in her seat. *A big dog? Who in town had a really big dog? And who would let it wander around by itself?*

"Do you really think this was done by a dog?" Cricket asked.

"This mess certainly was. A cougar usually covers its food, like what you and Shilo saw yesterday. Not this. It looks like something came along after that and made a mess." Her dad started the truck and headed toward home. "Maybe Jeremy got a picture."

Cricket hoped so. *Was Jeremy's data wrong? If it really was Elvis, what was going to happen to him?* she wondered. *Would he be killed? Or moved? What if it wasn't him? What if he was innocent?*

Chapter Five

"So, which is it?" Shilo demanded. "Is it a dog or a cougar?"

"Maybe both," Cricket said. She was lying on Shilo's bed, searching for cougar videos on her mom's phone.

"Well, Mrs. Steeves is convinced a cougar took Socks."

"Socks is missing? When did that happen?" Socks was an orange-and-white cat that lived next door to Shilo. Nothing scared Socks. The previous summer

Cricket and Shilo had watched him win a staring contest with a porcupine.

"Sometime after lunch yesterday, I think," Shilo said.

Cricket frowned. "That's a weird time for a cougar to be hunting. Are there any tracks?"

"I don't know."

Cricket sat up and put the phone in her pocket. "Let's go check it out."

* * *

Mrs. Steeves didn't shovel the snow off her deck very often. "This is perfect," Cricket said as she knelt in the snow.

"That looks just like the paw print Jeremy has!"

"Almost. But those are claw marks." Cricket took off her mitten and with her finger traced an X through the print. She dug the phone out of her pocket and took a photo. "That's not a cougar print. It's not Elvis."

"What's that in the snow?" Shilo pointed to a pile of something in the yard.

The girls followed the tracks.

Shilo wrinkled her nose. "Ew, it's poop!"

"That's great! Do you have a bag?" Cricket asked.

"What?" Shilo's eyes nearly bugged out of her head. "I'm not picking up that poop! You pick it up."

"Fine. Let's just take a picture."

"Taking pictures of cougar poop is kinda weird, even for you, Cricket."

"It's called scat when it's from an animal, Shilo, and I don't think it's from a cougar," Cricket said as she knelt down

to take a close-up photo. "A cougar is a cat, right? Cats usually cover their scat."

"It's not from a bear—they're all asleep."

Cricket nodded. "They should be."

"So what do you think it's from? Do you think it could be a wolf or a dog?"

Cricket paused. The back door of the cabin opened, and a gray head bristling with green curlers poked out. "What are you doing, girls? Have you found Socks?"

"Not yet, Mrs. Steeves. We're looking for some evidence," Shilo said.

"Well, you be careful now. I hear that cougar's been prowling around the café and nearly destroyed the garbage bin in the lane. Nothing's safe, not even poor Socks." Mrs. Steeves sniffled. "I sure hope your dad tells us his plan at the town meeting tonight, Cricket. Everyone wants to know what he's going to do about this cougar." Mrs. Steeves went back into the cabin and shut the door with a bang.

The girls looked at each other in dismay.

"It sounds like everyone thinks the cougar's to blame," Shilo said.

"Not me." Cricket pulled her mitten on. "Let's go check out the café."

* * *

Pearl's Café was right in the middle of town, and it was one of the few businesses that stayed open all year long. The girls followed the sound of hammering around the side of the building and into the back alley. Mrs. Chen was struggling to hold a board while she nailed it to the fence around the café's garbage bins.

"Can we help?" Cricket asked.

Mrs. Chen looked up in surprise. "You girls snuck up on me! I guess I'm a bit jumpy with a cougar wandering around. Just look at all the trouble he's caused."

She stepped back from the fence so the girls could see the dented garbage can.

"Are those teeth marks?" Shilo squeaked.

"Oh yes." Mrs. Chen nodded. "He's vicious, this one. And strong. Look what he did to my fence—and down at the Pizza Palace too."

Cricket looked down the alley and frowned. "The cougar knocked these fences down?"

"Why didn't he just jump them?" Shilo asked. "Jeremy said cougars can climb trees and stuff, so a fence shouldn't be a problem."

"What does a cougar think when he's hungry?" Mrs. Chen shook her head. "I don't know. I've been here fourteen years and never had this trouble. He's a bad one."

Cricket took her mom's phone out of her pocket and snapped pictures of the fence.

"This is really weird," she said, "but we can help you fix it."

Mrs. Chen smiled and gave Cricket the hammer. "You are very helpful, girls. Thank you. When you're done, come in for a cup of cocoa with marshmallows."

While they worked, Cricket worried about Elvis. *Was everyone convinced that a cougar was causing all this trouble in the town? Would they even consider another possibility—that Elvis might be innocent?*

Chapter Six

The entire town was at the meeting that night. Every seat in the campground amphitheater was filled. Warden McKay had a quick look at Cricket's photos but was too busy to talk with her. Cricket helped Jeremy unpack his equipment at the front of the room. When everything was ready, she perched on a stack of firewood at the side.

Warden McKay began the meeting by introducing Jeremy and reminding

everyone how to be safe in cougar territory.

"But I've worked in the park for eighteen years and only seen a cougar once," he said. "It was in the backcountry, up near Lineham Lakes. The cougar was acting like a cougar. It wasn't destroying garbage bins or stealing house cats."

"But there have been cougars in town before," Mrs. Steeves said from the front row.

Jeremy stepped forward. "I've been tracking the cougars in the park for a little while now," he said. He turned on the projector, and a map of the Waterton townsite filled the screen. "In the past two years one cougar has traveled through the town a few times on his way to Montana. The satellite data—these bright-green dots—show him sneaking

51

through in the very early morning, about four o'clock, when it's still dark."

"But what about *this* week? Do you have any more recent data?" Mr. Garrin asked from the back of the room. His tall black cowboy hat stood out in the crowd of winter hats.

"I do. This week he came through and farther into town than usual," Jeremy said. "That was the day before yesterday. But he's been nowhere near Mrs. Steeves's cabin or the back of the café. Or the stables."

Mr. Garrin snorted. "Maybe it's a cat you don't have a collar on," he said.

Cricket saw several people nodding. They looked worried.

"That would be unusual. Cougars are solitary and very territorial." Jeremy changed the screen to a night-vision picture. The photo was in shades of gray, with two bright spots deep in the bush. It took Cricket a moment to recognize it as the bush in the schoolyard.

"There it is! In the bushes!" People leaned forward trying to see.

Jeremy shook his head. "There's something there, but we didn't get a clear picture of it. I don't think it's a cougar."

"What else could it be?" someone asked.

"It's a cougar. I know it," someone else said loudly.

Cricket wanted to jump up and tell them about the giant dog tracks, but everyone looked very upset. No one was going to listen to her right now.

Warden McKay held up his hand, and slowly the townsfolk grew quiet. "We're going to use Jeremy's dogs and track the cougar. Once we catch him, we'll move him into a new territory far from town."

Oh no! Cricket jumped off the stack of firewood. Her dad had told her relocation didn't work the same way for cougars as it did for bears. Moving Elvis could put him right in the middle of another cougar's territory and cause a deadly fight.

Many people were nodding now. They were happy that something was being done.

They're all convinced it's a cougar, Cricket thought. *Elvis is doomed.*

Chapter Seven

The next morning Warden McKay went out with Jeremy and the dogs before dawn. Cricket prowled around the house restlessly. Finally, at lunchtime, she heard her dad stomping the snow from his boots before he came in the back door. She held his radio and thick gloves as he pulled off his winter coat.

"We didn't find him," he said. "The dogs couldn't find any signs of a cougar at all."

Cricket let out a sigh. "That's good, right?"

"Well, it would be, except something's spooking Mr. Garrin's horses at the stables. They kicked up a ruckus last night and again this morning."

Cricket frowned. "Is it a different cougar?"

"Jeremy doesn't think so. If there was a new cougar trying to establish his territory here, we should have found plenty of signs of it. It should have been easy for the dogs to smell," he said as he sat down at the table with a stack of papers and files. "Whatever it is, this animal has caused more trouble than all the bears we had in August."

* * *

Cricket couldn't sit still, and it didn't take much to convince Tyler and Shilo to walk down to Pat's Garage.

"I've sure been selling a lot of ice cream this week," Pat said, handing

Cricket her change and a napkin for her ice-cream sandwich.

The girls scanned the magazines and listened to the conversation in the store. So many people had stories that it seemed as though the cougar had been taking a tour of the town, stopping to cause trouble at nearly every house and business.

"First a deer, then a house cat—it won't be long before a person is attacked," Mr. Garrin said, pushing up the brim of his cowboy hat.

Mrs. Steeves stepped up to the counter with a carton of milk. "Oh, do you mean Socks?" Her cheeks grew pink. "I guess you didn't hear. Socks is fine. He must have been hiding. Probably scared to death of that cougar."

Cricket looked at Shilo in surprise. Shilo shrugged. She hadn't heard this either.

"You know, cougar attacks on humans are very rare. In fact, there have been fewer than thirty attacks on humans in the last hundred years." Everyone in the store turned to look at Tyler. "That's in Canada, of course. The stats are a bit different in the United States."

Cricket rolled her eyes. Tyler was such a know-it-all. Obviously he had been researching cougars, even though school was still canceled.

"A cougar stalks its prey or waits for it to come to him. He has to catch it in two or three jumps. He doesn't like to chase it. He'll hunt just about anything if he's hungry enough. He'll even eat a porcupine—quills and everything—if he catches one."

Mr. Garrin snorted in disbelief.

"Maybe your dad will set up a trap," Pat suggested.

Tyler shrugged. "Maybe. Traps aren't used to catch cougars in Alberta anymore. They're shot with tranquilizers. But he could try to use one of the bear traps, I guess."

"If that trap can catch a cougar or a bear, it could catch a dog too, right?" Cricket asked.

"You mean like a wolf?" Tyler asked.

Mr. Garrin snorted again. "There hasn't been a wolf seen around town for years."

"Not a wolf," Cricket said, pulling her mom's phone from her pocket. "I think it's a dog, a really big dog. See these tracks?"

Pat raised his eyebrows, then shook his head. Mrs. Steeves glanced at the picture and patted Cricket on the shoulder.

Cricket sighed. They wouldn't believe it could be a dog until they saw it. But Tyler had given her an idea. She moved to the back of the store and searched the shelves.

"Why are you looking at dog food?" Shilo asked.

Cricket pointed to the cans of food. "Which one do you think will be the smelliest?"

"That's easy. This tuna one will be really stinky. But you don't have a dog."

Cricket shook her head.

Shilo's eyebrows went up. "But you have a plan?"

Cricket nodded. *Yes, she did have a plan.*

Chapter Eight

"What do you mean, you *sort of* remember how to do it?" Cricket asked.

"I only saw Dad do it once," Tyler said. "But I think it's stuck."

Cricket handed Shilo her backpack. "Do you think it's frozen shut?" She took her mitten off so she could get a better grip on the handle of the drawer. The metal nearly froze her fingers.

The girls had convinced Tyler to go with them to the warden station. Instead of going inside, they had snuck around the building to the bear trap parked near the trees. The big white culvert trap was shaped like a giant metal tube lying on its side. Each end was covered with strong metal mesh. The bait drawer was near one end. This was where Cricket would place the dog food—if they could get the drawer open.

"Argh! I can't get it." Cricket put her mitten back on. "Now what?"

All three kids looked at the trap, thinking. "I guess someone has to crawl inside to set the bait," Tyler said finally.

"Not me!" Shilo said. "I'm not crawling into that thing. What if *I* get stuck in there?"

"Me neither," Tyler said.

They looked at Cricket. It was her idea, so she was going to have to do the dirty work.

"I'll open the door for you," Tyler said. He wrapped both hands around the long metal lever on the side of the trap and used his whole body to pull it down. The huge mesh door on the end of the trap rose. The frozen metal squealed.

"Okay, Cricket. You can go in now," Tyler said.

Cricket took a deep breath, then climbed up into the trap. She covered her nose with her mitten. She had expected the trap to smell like bears, but it was *really* smelly, like a cage at the zoo. She turned around and tried to stand up. Her head hit the top of the trap.

"Ouch!"

"Are you okay?" Shilo stood a few feet away, watching.

"Yeah. Do you have the dog food?"

Shilo opened the can. "Pee-yew!" she said, holding her mitten over her nose. She passed the can through the door quickly, as though afraid the trap would slam down on her arm.

Cricket crawled on her hands and knees to the other end of the trap. She set the dog food on the pressure sensor in the bait drawer.

"What if the sensor is frozen too?" she called.

"Maybe you should test it," Tyler called back.

"How?"

"Take the food off the sensor."

Cricket lifted the can, and the metal door slammed closed with a bang. The whole trap shook. Cricket squeaked and dropped the can.

"Oh no! Cricket, are you okay?" Shilo peered into the trap. "Great idea, Tyler. What if you can't get it open again? What if she's stuck in there?"

Cricket's heart pounded. "I'm okay, but I spilled some of the food."

Tyler poked his head over Shilo's shoulder and grinned at Cricket. "Now we know it works," he said. He ducked a jab from Shilo's elbow and went back to the lever. "Don't put the bait on the sensor until the door is up."

"Sure thing, genius," Cricket said.

The door squealed again as it rose. Cricket carefully placed the can back on the sensor, then crawled to the opening of the trap. She looked up. The door was steady. She crouched and then sprang out of the trap and into the snow.

"Yay!" Shilo cheered.

They gathered their backpacks and headed home.

"Do you really expect to catch a dog, Cricket?" Tyler asked. "I mean, with all the wild animals in the park, do you really think you'll catch a dog in that trap? Right next to the warden station?"

Cricket nodded. "He's starving," she said. "He can probably smell that stinky dog food from the other side of town. You'll see."

Chapter Nine

The kids were halfway home when the big white National Park Warden truck pulled up beside them.

Warden McKay rolled down his window. "Do you kids want a ride home?"

"Yes, please!" Cricket said. She and Shilo climbed in the passenger side, and Tyler jumped into the back seat. They did up their seat belts just as the radio squawked.

"Warden McKay, this is headquarters. What is your location? Over."

Cricket's dad picked up the radio. "I'm in the village, Sarah. What's up?"

"The trap alarm just went off again. That's twice in the past half hour. Did you set the bear trap, sir?"

Warden McKay rested the radio on his knee. He seemed puzzled.

"Sir? Do you want me to go out and check on it?" Sarah asked.

"No, I'll come back right now. It's probably just a malfunction."

"Ten-four."

Warden McKay returned the radio to the console and glanced at the girls. They couldn't hide their excitement. "Okay, what's up? Do you know something about that trap?"

Cricket nodded. Her dad's face changed from puzzled to worried to angry. After he finished telling them how dangerous the trap was and that tampering with the trap was illegal, he took a deep breath and turned the truck around.

Tyler leaned over the seat. "Do you really think the trap malfunctioned, Dad? Do you think it could be a cougar?"

"I don't know what to think, Tyler."

"It's not even dusk," Cricket said. "Cougars don't hunt at this time of day."

"Maybe he couldn't resist the bait," Shilo said. "Maybe he's starving."

"Or maybe it caught something else," Cricket said. She crossed her fingers inside her mittens.

When Warden McKay parked the truck, the headlights shone into the trap. The mesh door was down, and the light only shone in partway. The back of the trap was pitch black. They all sat and watched for a minute. Nothing happened. They rolled the windows down. Silence.

"You kids stay here while I check it," Cricket's dad said as he climbed out of the truck. The kids watched as he unlocked his rifle and checked that it was loaded. This wasn't an adventure anymore—it was serious.

Cricket held her breath.

"Do you think there's something in there?" Shilo asked.

Cricket nodded. She leaned forward. "Did you see that?"

"What? What did you see?" Shilo stared hard into the dark trap.

"See the eyes, there at the back. Did you see that?"

"No, Cricket, I—"

Loud angry barking erupted at the back of the trap. Both girls jumped in their seats. Tyler banged his head on the back window. Warden McKay jumped away from the trap. A huge animal charged at the mesh door, barking and snarling.

"That's not a cougar," Shilo squeaked.

"It's not a wolf either," Tyler said.

The giant dog stood at the door with its head down, growling. Bits of slobber streaked its black snout and sprayed the brown fur on its shoulders.

"I've never seen such a big dog," Shilo said.

"But I can see his ribs," Cricket said. "No wonder he climbed into the trap for the bait. He *is* starving."

The dog had stopped growling. He quivered, but Cricket couldn't tell if he was angry or afraid.

Warden McKay returned to the truck. "I think you might have caught the troublemaker. I bet the cougar is miles away from here."

That evening Cricket, Shilo and Tyler walked over to Jeremy's cabin.

"What did you want to show us?" Cricket asked as they took off their boots and coats.

"I've found Elvis," Jeremy said.

Cricket's heart jumped. "He's not in town again, is he?"

"You haven't told anyone, have you?" Shilo asked.

Jeremy held up his hands. "Whoa, he's nowhere near town. In fact, he hasn't been around for a couple of days." He turned and pointed to the map on his computer screen.

Tyler leaned forward and studied the map. "That looks like Crandell Mountain. And this could be Red Rock Canyon."

Jeremy nodded. "That's right. He went through the canyon late last night, then continued west. It looks like Elvis is trying to get away from Waterton as fast as he can."

Cricket sighed with relief.

"It had to take him at least a day to get that far," Jeremy said. "He must have been heading out of town when he followed the snowshoers on that trail."

"Which means he couldn't have done any of those things in town," Cricket said.

"Except kill a deer—and hide it right in our schoolyard!" Shilo said.

"True, but after that he was gone. He didn't cause any of the other problems," Cricket said.

"You were right all along, Cricket. The town really did catch a bad case of phantom frenzy," Jeremy said.

"I'm glad he got away okay, but I kind of wish I had seen him, even for just a second."

Jeremy smiled and picked up a folder from his desk. "I know it's not quite the same thing, but I printed these for you." He handed each of them a large night-vision photo of a trail deep in the woods, lit by a carpet of white snow. In the middle of the picture, staring right into the camera, was Elvis. His front paw was raised as though he had paused in midstride. His eyes glowed brightly.

Cricket grinned. This was better than seeing Elvis in town, where he was in danger. In the forest he was at home and safe.

Epilogue

Cougars do exist in Waterton Lakes National Park and elsewhere within North America, though they are rarely seen. Collaring animals such as bears and cougars is one way scientists can follow an animal's movements and determine the size of its range, and the collaring techniques described in the story are actually used by scientists studying cougars. Just a decade ago the collar had to fall off the animal before data could be gathered. Today improvements in GPS (Global Positioning Systems) and remote data gathering enable scientists to track a cougar in real time, seeing where it is going as it is moving.

Cougars are at the top of their food chain, so by studying them scientists are able to evaluate the overall health of an ecosystem. A rise in the cougar population means there is an abundance of prey animals, such as deer, elk and moose, as well as smaller prey like hares, grouse and even porcupines. But a rise in the cougar population also means that young cougars must travel farther in their search for unoccupied territory, sometimes bringing them into contact with human populations.

In 2005 it was estimated there were only 680 cougars in Alberta. In 2015 that number had risen to more than 2,000. By studying cougars, scientists hope to understand how humans, livestock and cougars can coexist.

Pamela McDowell's first career was in education, teaching junior high and high school. She began writing when she left teaching and has now written more than fifty nonfiction books for children. Her three previous early chapter books focusing on Cricket and her life in Waterton Lakes National Park were all CCBC Best Books. Pamela grew up in Alberta and enjoys writing about the diverse animals and habitats of her home province. She lives in Calgary with her husband, two kids and an Australian shepherd. *Cougar Frenzy* is the fourth book featuring Cricket and her friends.

DON'T MISS THE
LARK BA
DETECTIVE SERIES